The Arabian Cinderella
and the Secret of the Woven Threads

by Dr. Hamsa Mahafza

DORRANCE
PUBLISHING CO
EST. 1920
PITTSBURGH, PENNSYLVANIA 15238

The contents of this work, including, but not limited to, the accuracy of events, people, and places depicted; opinions expressed; illustrations, ideas; permission to use previously published materials included; and any advice given or actions advocated are solely the responsibility of the author, who assumes all liability for said work and indemnifies the publisher against any claims stemming from publication of the work.

All Rights Reserved
Copyright © 2022 by Dr. Hamsa Mahafza

No part of this book may be reproduced or transmitted, downloaded, distributed, reverse engineered, or stored in or introduced into any information storage and retrieval system, in any form or by any means, including photocopying and recording, whether electronic or mechanical, now known or hereinafter invented without permission in writing from the publisher.

Dorrance Publishing Co
585 Alpha Drive
Suite 103
Pittsburgh, PA 15238
Visit our website at *www.dorrancebookstore.com*

ISBN: 979-8-88729-993-8
eISBN: 979-8-88729-718-7

The Arabian Cinderella
and the Secret of the Woven Threads

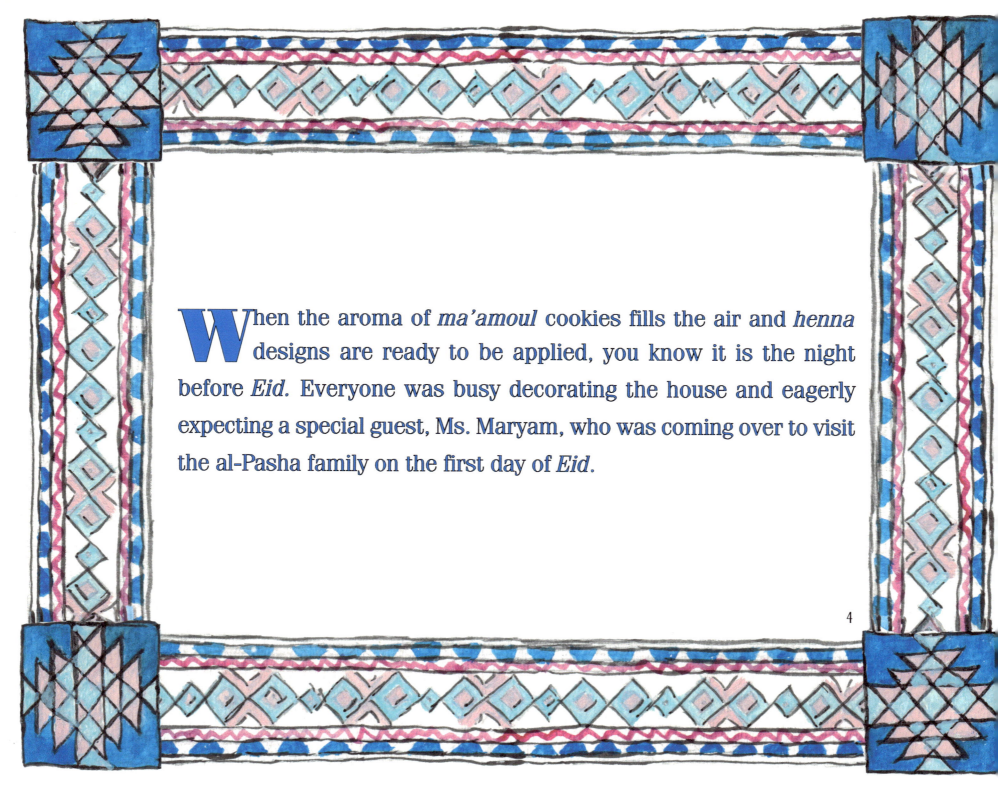

When the aroma of *ma'amoul* cookies fills the air and *henna* designs are ready to be applied, you know it is the night before *Eid*. Everyone was busy decorating the house and eagerly expecting a special guest, Ms. Maryam, who was coming over to visit the al-Pasha family on the first day of *Eid*.

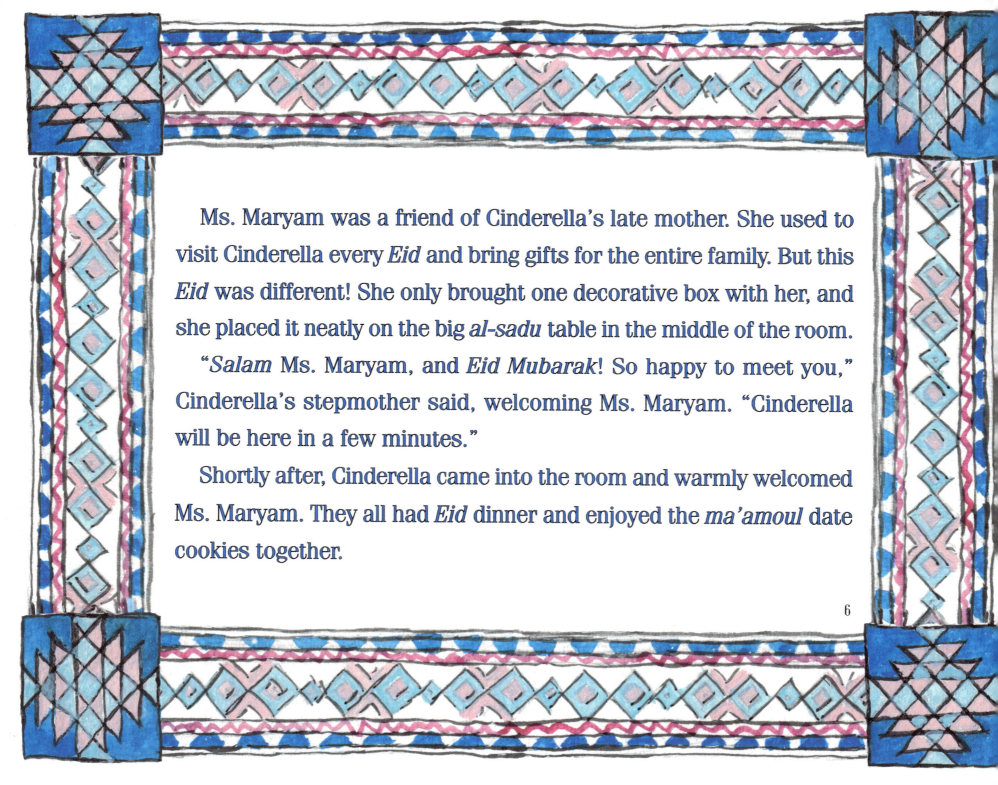

Ms. Maryam was a friend of Cinderella's late mother. She used to visit Cinderella every *Eid* and bring gifts for the entire family. But this *Eid* was different! She only brought one decorative box with her, and she placed it neatly on the big *al-sadu* table in the middle of the room.

"*Salam* Ms. Maryam, and *Eid Mubarak*! So happy to meet you," Cinderella's stepmother said, welcoming Ms. Maryam. "Cinderella will be here in a few minutes."

Shortly after, Cinderella came into the room and warmly welcomed Ms. Maryam. They all had *Eid* dinner and enjoyed the *ma'amoul* date cookies together.

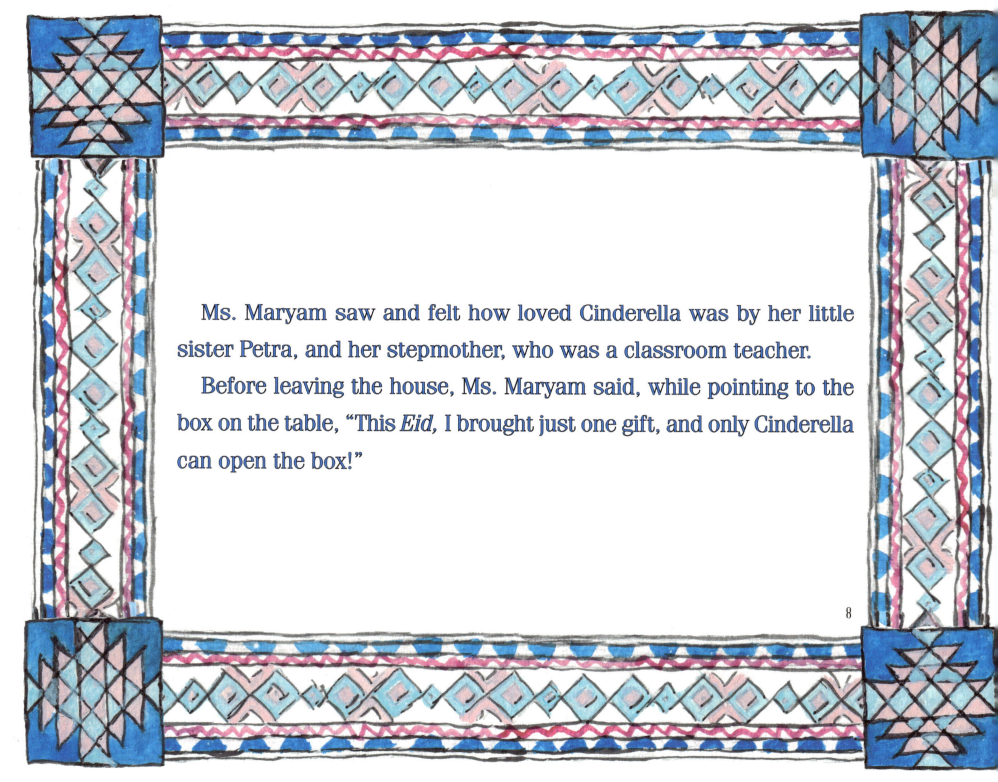

Ms. Maryam saw and felt how loved Cinderella was by her little sister Petra, and her stepmother, who was a classroom teacher.

Before leaving the house, Ms. Maryam said, while pointing to the box on the table, "This *Eid,* I brought just one gift, and only Cinderella can open the box!"

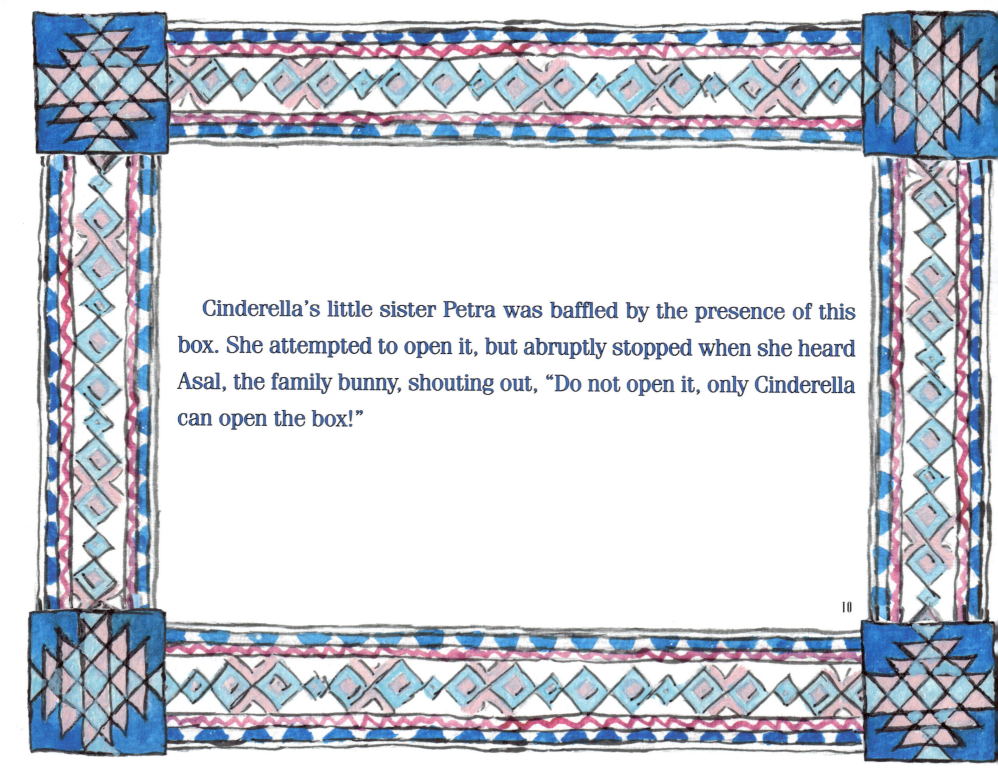

Cinderella's little sister Petra was baffled by the presence of this box. She attempted to open it, but abruptly stopped when she heard Asal, the family bunny, shouting out, "Do not open it, only Cinderella can open the box!"

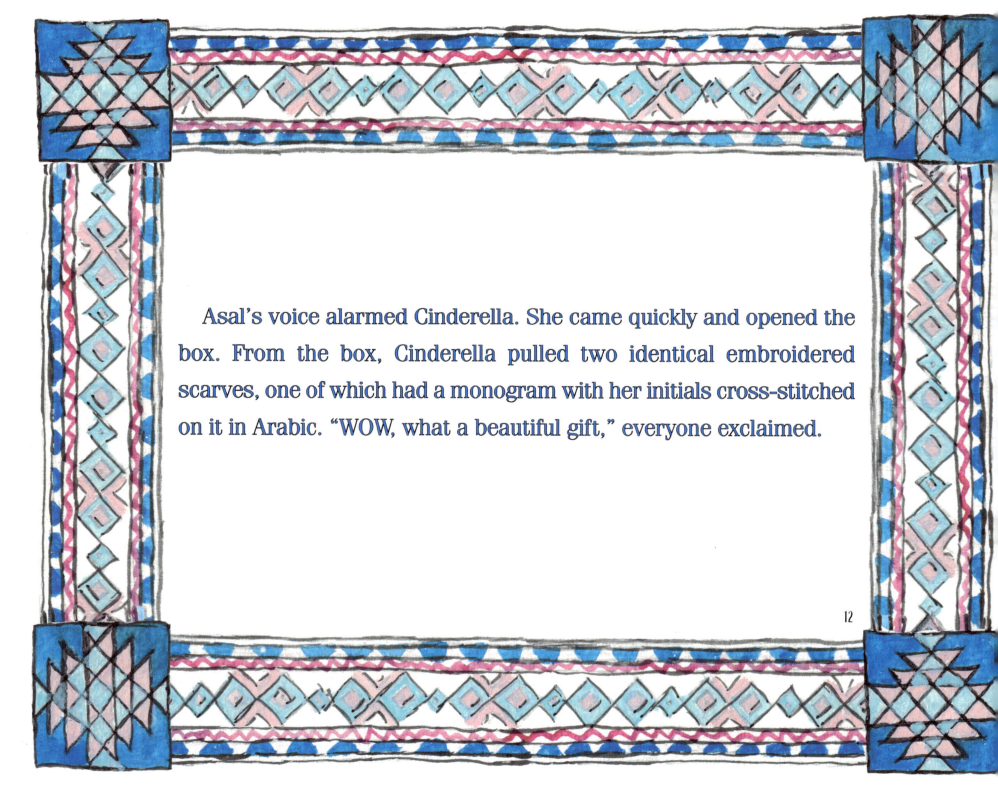

Asal's voice alarmed Cinderella. She came quickly and opened the box. From the box, Cinderella pulled two identical embroidered scarves, one of which had a monogram with her initials cross-stitched on it in Arabic. "WOW, what a beautiful gift," everyone exclaimed.

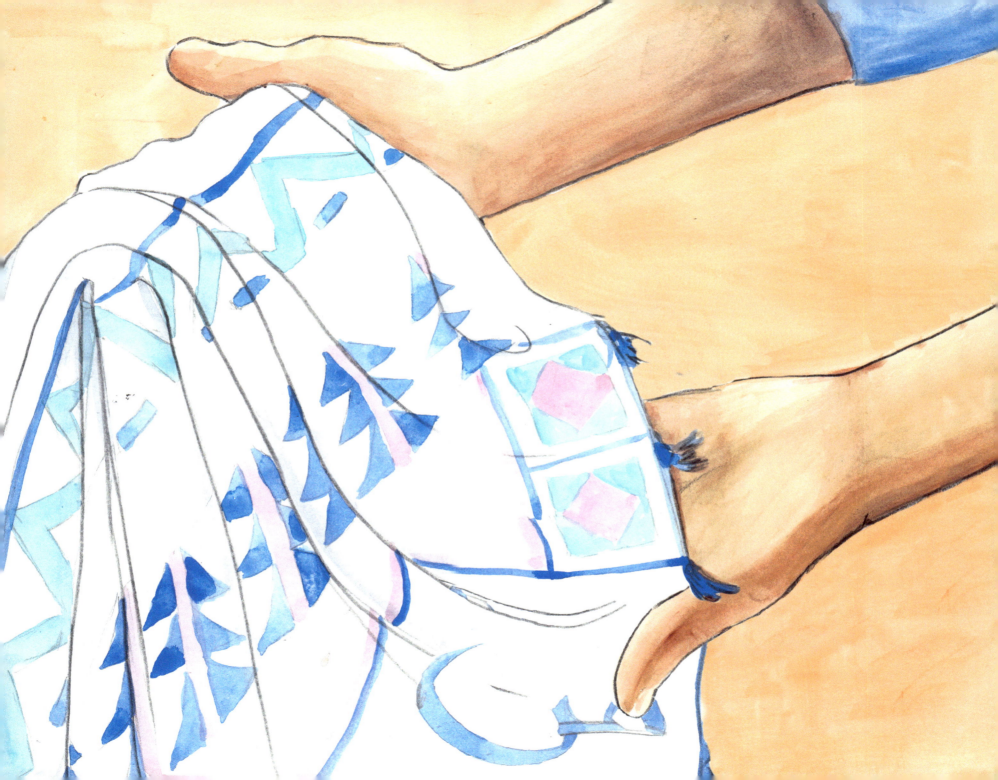

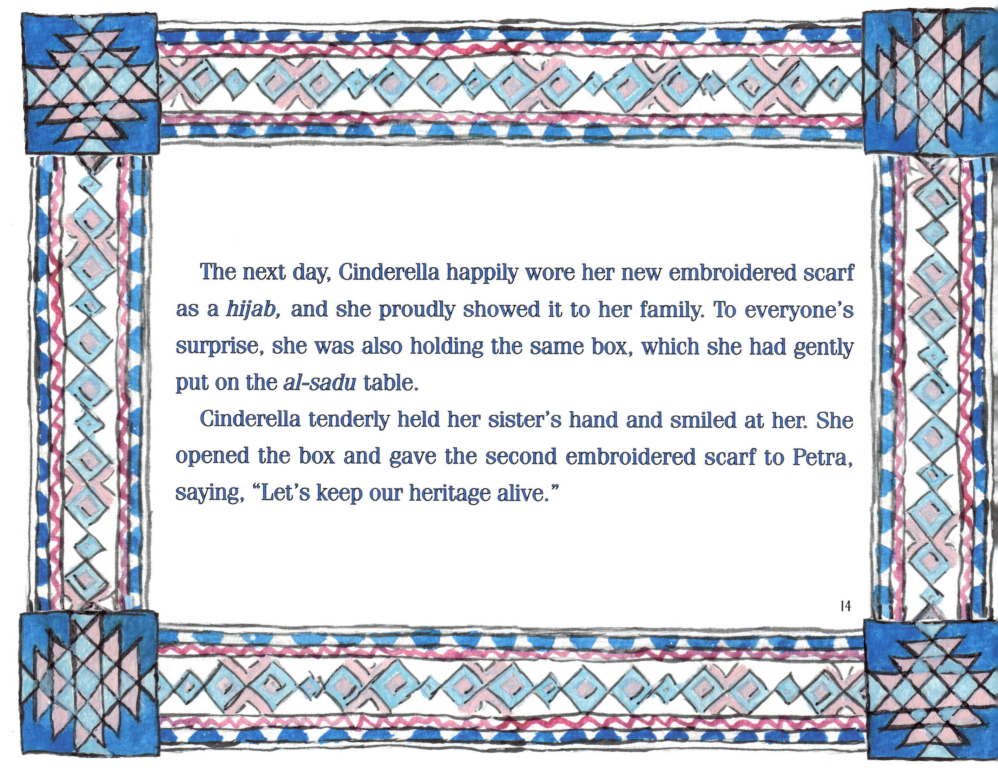

The next day, Cinderella happily wore her new embroidered scarf as a *hijab,* and she proudly showed it to her family. To everyone's surprise, she was also holding the same box, which she had gently put on the *al-sadu* table.

Cinderella tenderly held her sister's hand and smiled at her. She opened the box and gave the second embroidered scarf to Petra, saying, "Let's keep our heritage alive."

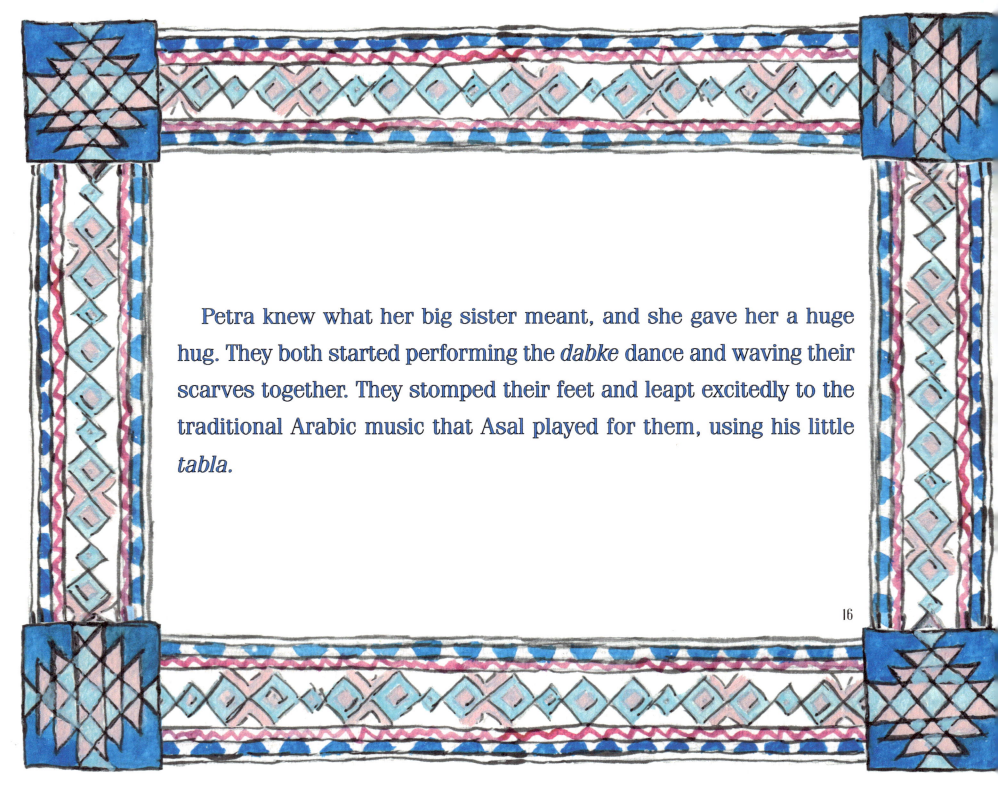

Petra knew what her big sister meant, and she gave her a huge hug. They both started performing the *dabke* dance and waving their scarves together. They stomped their feet and leapt excitedly to the traditional Arabic music that Asal played for them, using his little *tabla*.

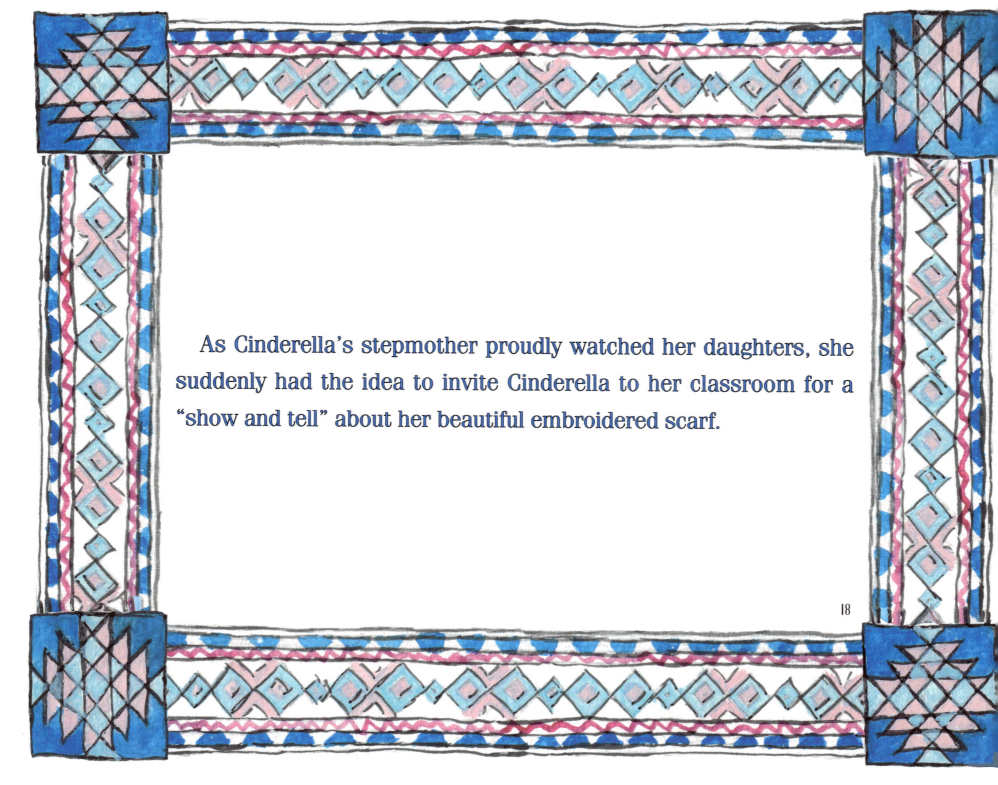

As Cinderella's stepmother proudly watched her daughters, she suddenly had the idea to invite Cinderella to her classroom for a "show and tell" about her beautiful embroidered scarf.

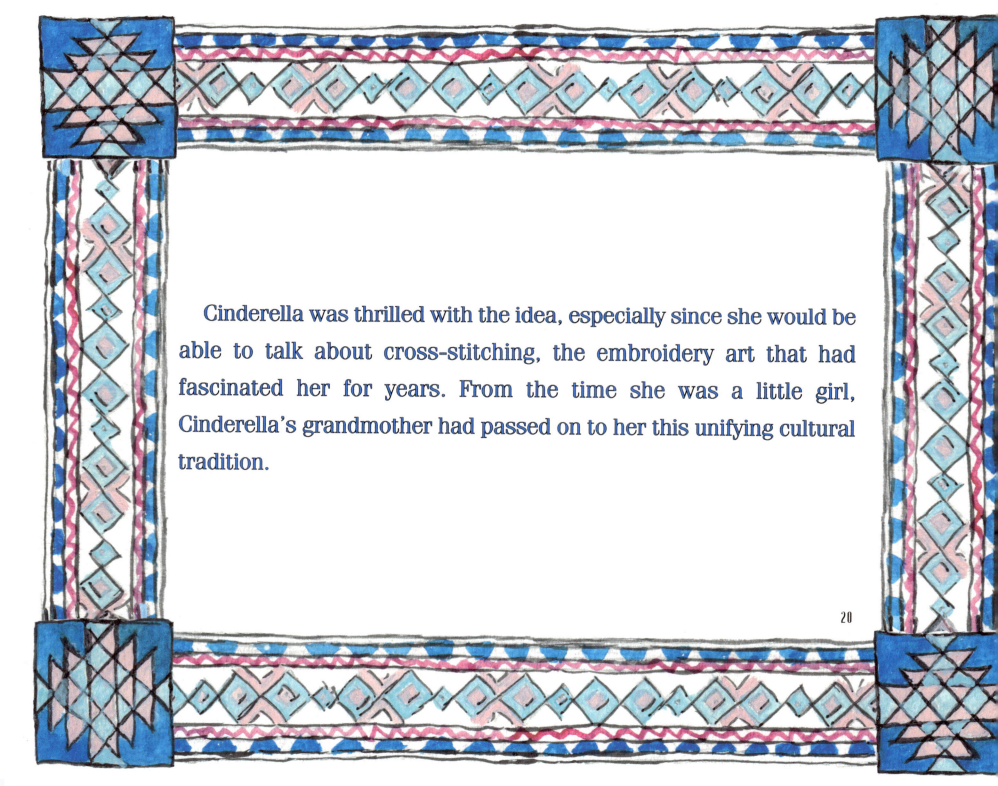

Cinderella was thrilled with the idea, especially since she would be able to talk about cross-stitching, the embroidery art that had fascinated her for years. From the time she was a little girl, Cinderella's grandmother had passed on to her this unifying cultural tradition.

The next day at her stepmother's classroom, the first thing Cinderella told the students was, "Through embroidery we can keep our heritage alive." All of the students' eyes were focused on Cinderella, wondering what she meant by keeping their "heritage alive."

Cinderella gestured to the box that she had placed on the teacher's table and said: "We all can do things to help keep our heritage alive. The secret is inside this box."

All the boys and girls were eagerly listening to Cinderella, except one student who quietly tried to open the box but was quickly interrupted as Asal the bunny jumped and shouted loudly, "Only Cinderella can open the box!"

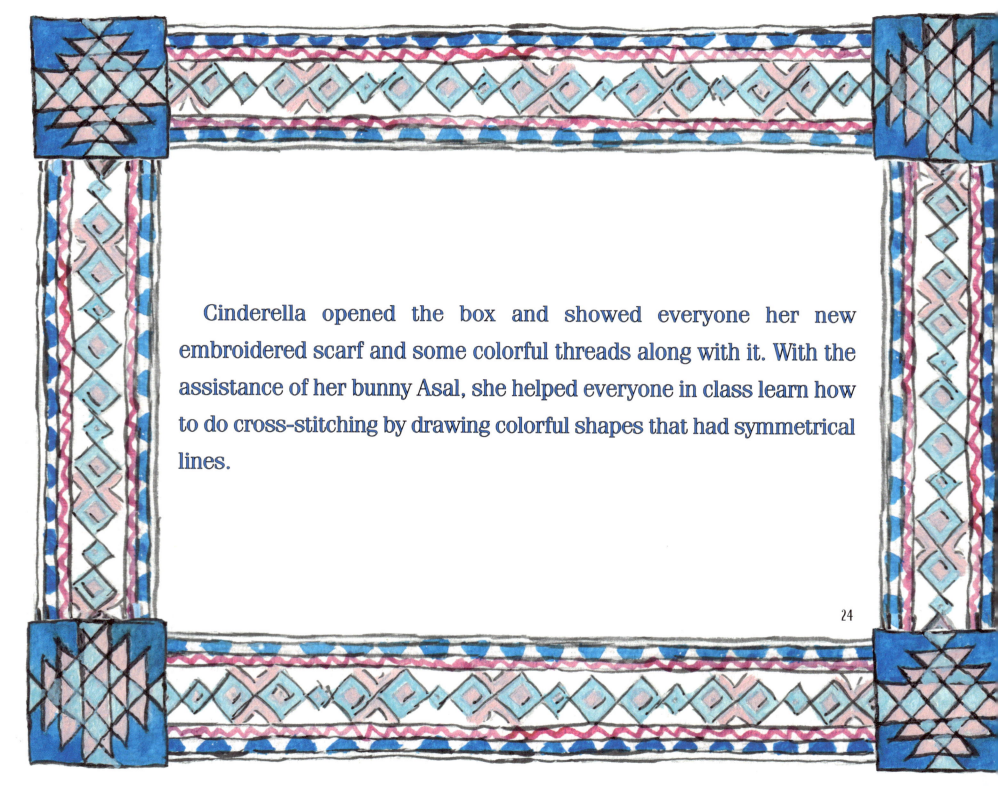

Cinderella opened the box and showed everyone her new embroidered scarf and some colorful threads along with it. With the assistance of her bunny Asal, she helped everyone in class learn how to do cross-stitching by drawing colorful shapes that had symmetrical lines.

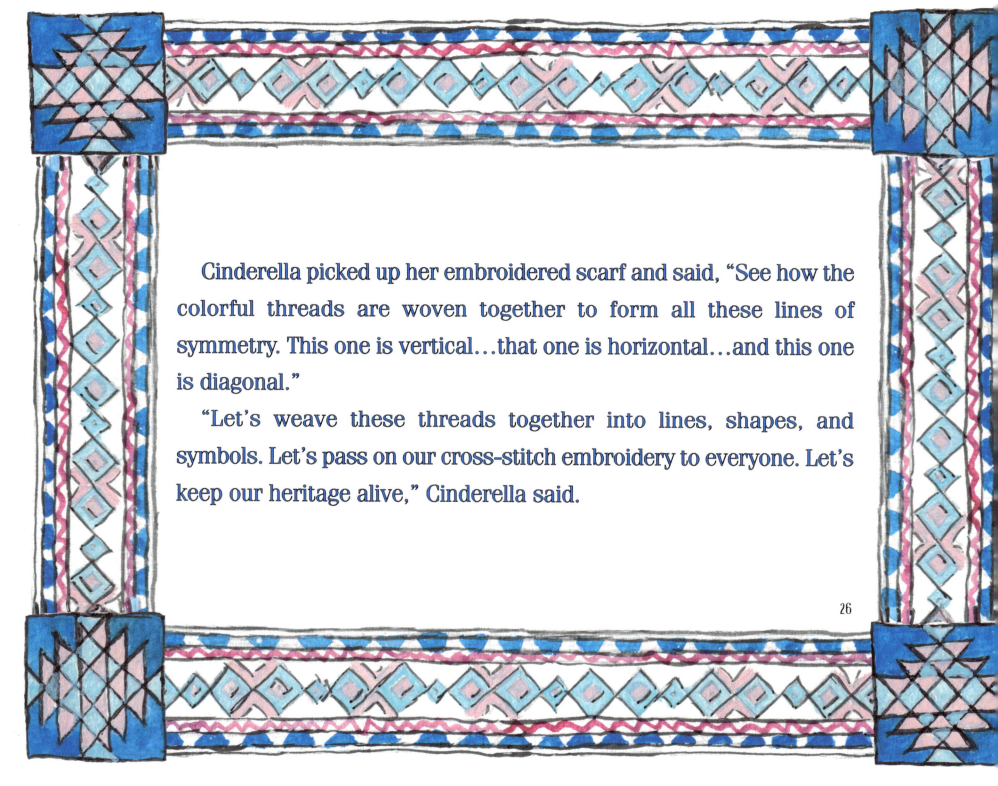

Cinderella picked up her embroidered scarf and said, "See how the colorful threads are woven together to form all these lines of symmetry. This one is vertical…that one is horizontal…and this one is diagonal."

"Let's weave these threads together into lines, shapes, and symbols. Let's pass on our cross-stitch embroidery to everyone. Let's keep our heritage alive," Cinderella said.

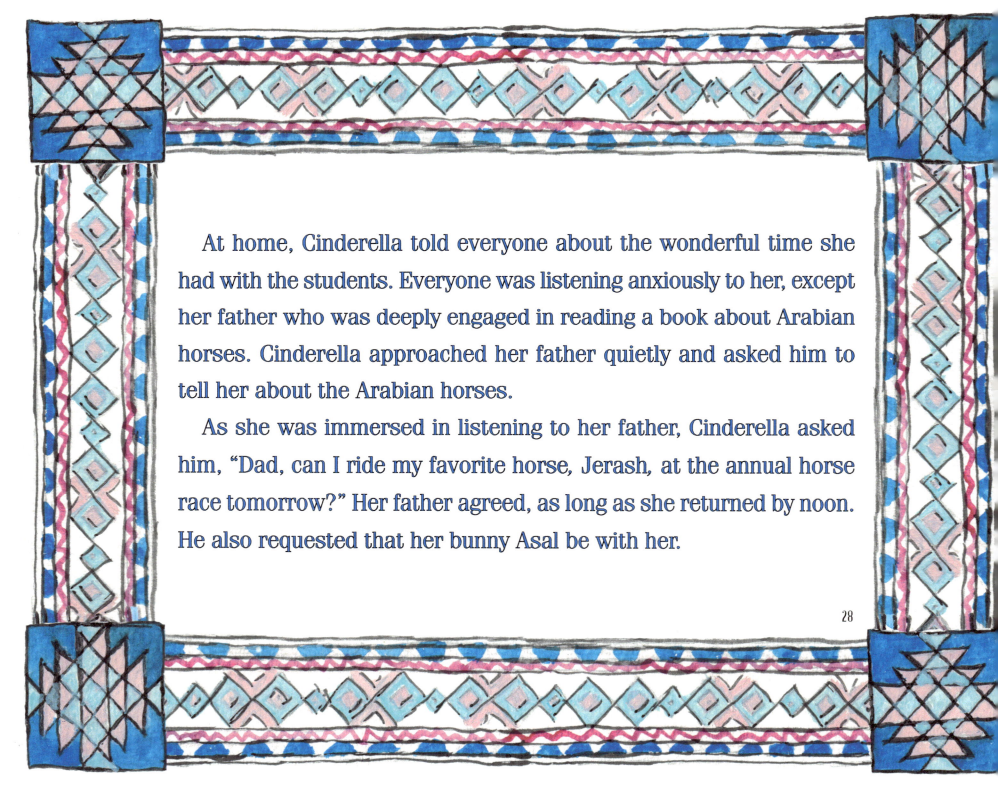

At home, Cinderella told everyone about the wonderful time she had with the students. Everyone was listening anxiously to her, except her father who was deeply engaged in reading a book about Arabian horses. Cinderella approached her father quietly and asked him to tell her about the Arabian horses.

As she was immersed in listening to her father, Cinderella asked him, "Dad, can I ride my favorite horse, Jerash, at the annual horse race tomorrow?" Her father agreed, as long as she returned by noon. He also requested that her bunny Asal be with her.

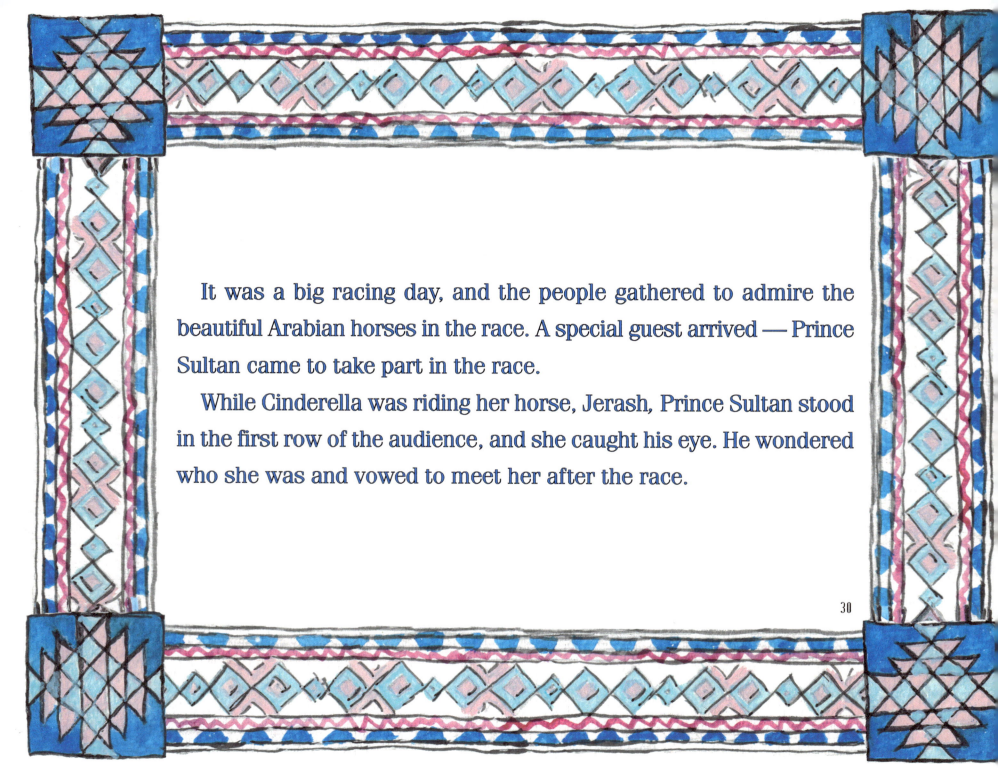

It was a big racing day, and the people gathered to admire the beautiful Arabian horses in the race. A special guest arrived — Prince Sultan came to take part in the race.

While Cinderella was riding her horse, Jerash, Prince Sultan stood in the first row of the audience, and she caught his eye. He wondered who she was and vowed to meet her after the race.

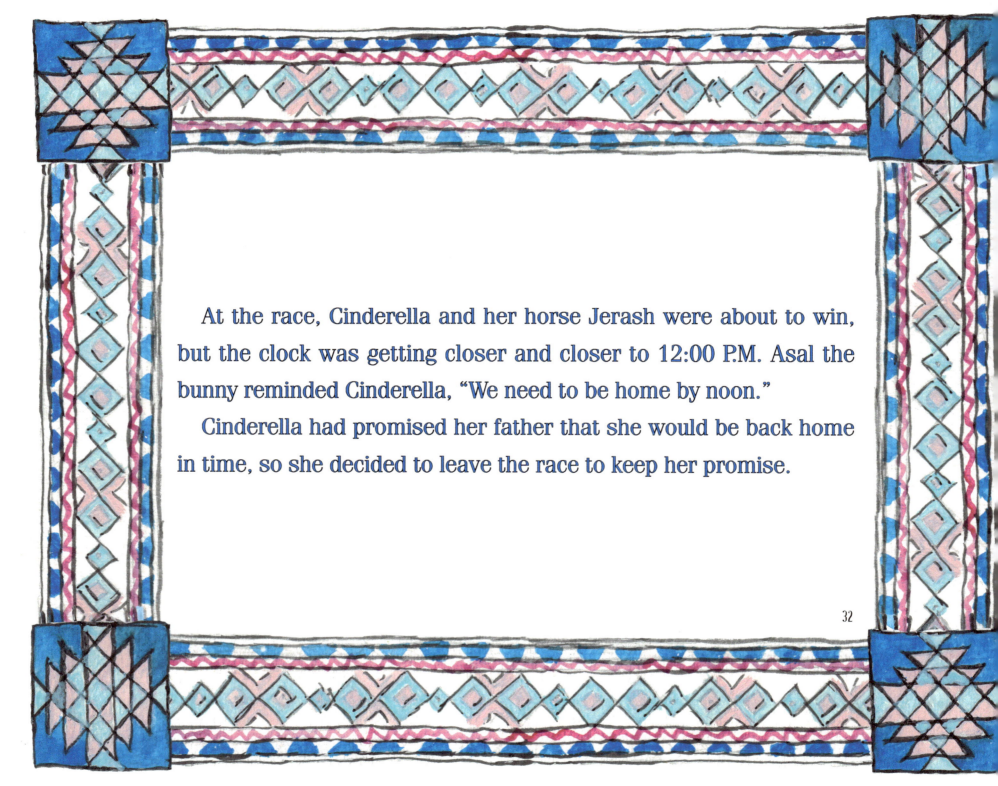

At the race, Cinderella and her horse Jerash were about to win, but the clock was getting closer and closer to 12:00 P.M. Asal the bunny reminded Cinderella, "We need to be home by noon."

Cinderella had promised her father that she would be back home in time, so she decided to leave the race to keep her promise.

As Cinderella was turning to leave, a tree branch snagged her embroidered headscarf, ripping off the square piece with her Arabic initials on it.

After the race, Prince Sultan searched and searched everywhere, but he couldn't find Cinderella. Finally, he looked in the distance, and he caught a glimpse of her just as she was running away. He tried to catch up to her, but she was too far, and she slipped out of sight.

Discouraged, Prince Sultan walked back to the race track. But on his way, he found the piece of Cinderella's scarf bearing her initials.

Cinderella arrived home just a little before the clock struck 12:00 P.M. She was happy that she was on time, just as she had promised her dad, though her heart was broken because a piece was torn off of her beautiful scarf.

While everyone was trying to comfort her, her little sister Petra brought over the scarf that Cinderella had gifted to her. Petra whispered softly in her big sister's ear, "When we share our gifts together, we can also keep our heritage alive."

Many days passed, and Cinderella was still missing the piece of her scarf. She was sad. She felt she had lost a precious part of her culture.

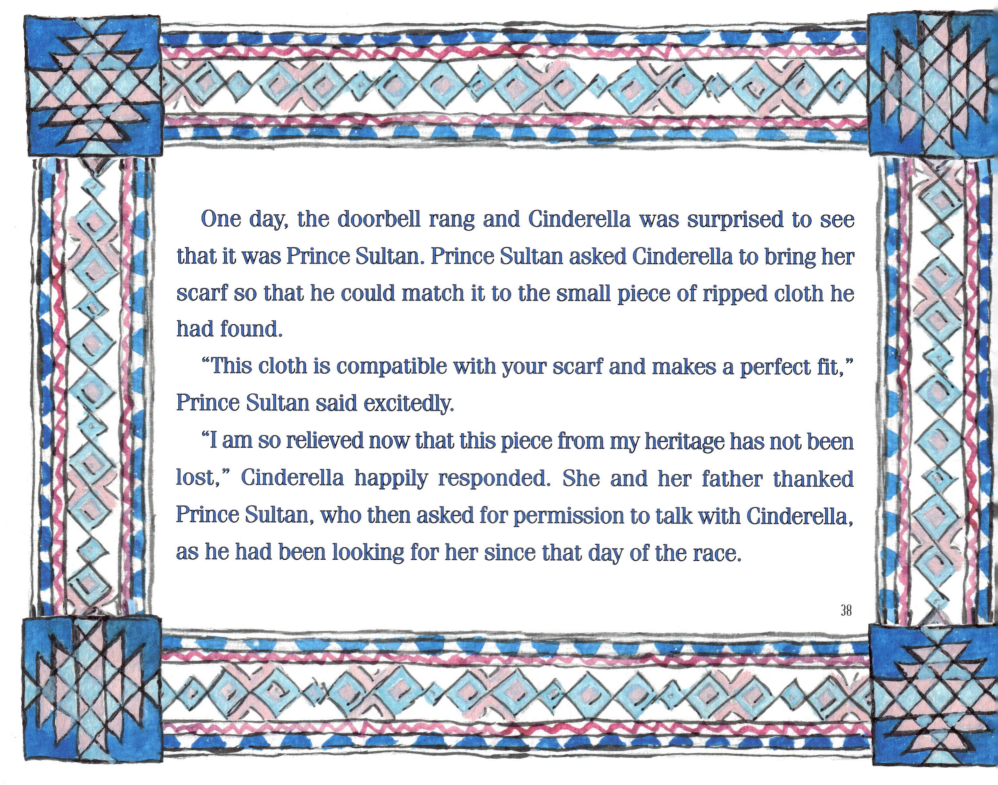

One day, the doorbell rang and Cinderella was surprised to see that it was Prince Sultan. Prince Sultan asked Cinderella to bring her scarf so that he could match it to the small piece of ripped cloth he had found.

"This cloth is compatible with your scarf and makes a perfect fit," Prince Sultan said excitedly.

"I am so relieved now that this piece from my heritage has not been lost," Cinderella happily responded. She and her father thanked Prince Sultan, who then asked for permission to talk with Cinderella, as he had been looking for her since that day of the race.

"Cinderella, would you like to talk with the Prince?" her father asked. Cinderella agreed. She looked at the Prince and found him to be a kind man. She was impressed that he had spent so much time looking for her to give her the missing piece of her scarf.

Afterwards, the Prince and his family started visiting Cinderella and her family. A beautiful relationship blossomed between them. Cinderella and Prince Sultan shared a common love of their heritage, and they promised each other to keep it alive.

A little while later, Cinderella and the Prince were to be married, and the two families gave their blessings. Prince Sultan wanted to surprise Cinderella with a new scarf to replace the one that was torn at the annual horse race on the first day he met her.

On the *henna* night, the women's party before the wedding, Prince Sultan gifted Cinderella a fancy box with a beautiful, embroidered scarf inside it. He asked her little sister Petra to place the box on the big *al-sadu* table in the middle of the living room.

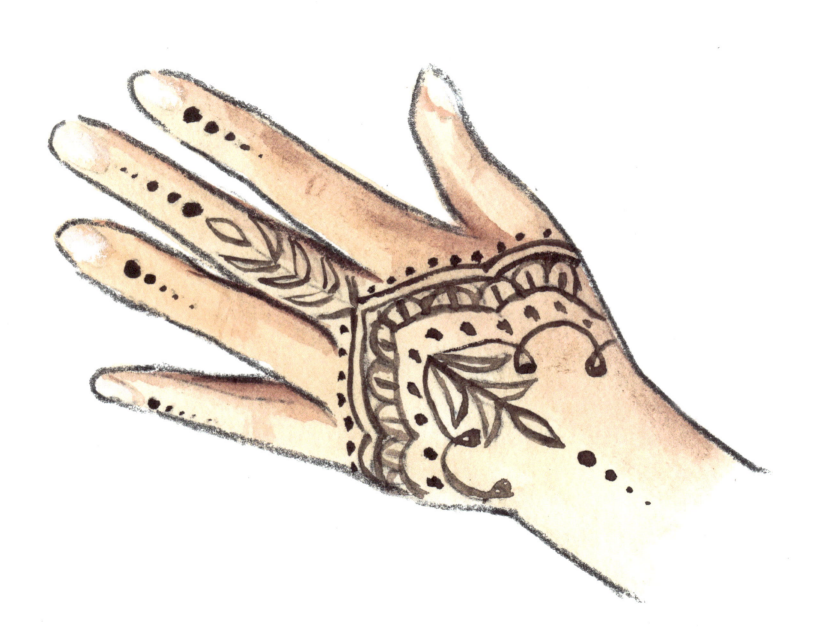

Sure enough, when Petra saw the box, she wanted to open it! Guess what happened next? Asal the bunny shouted, "Only Cinderella can open the box!"

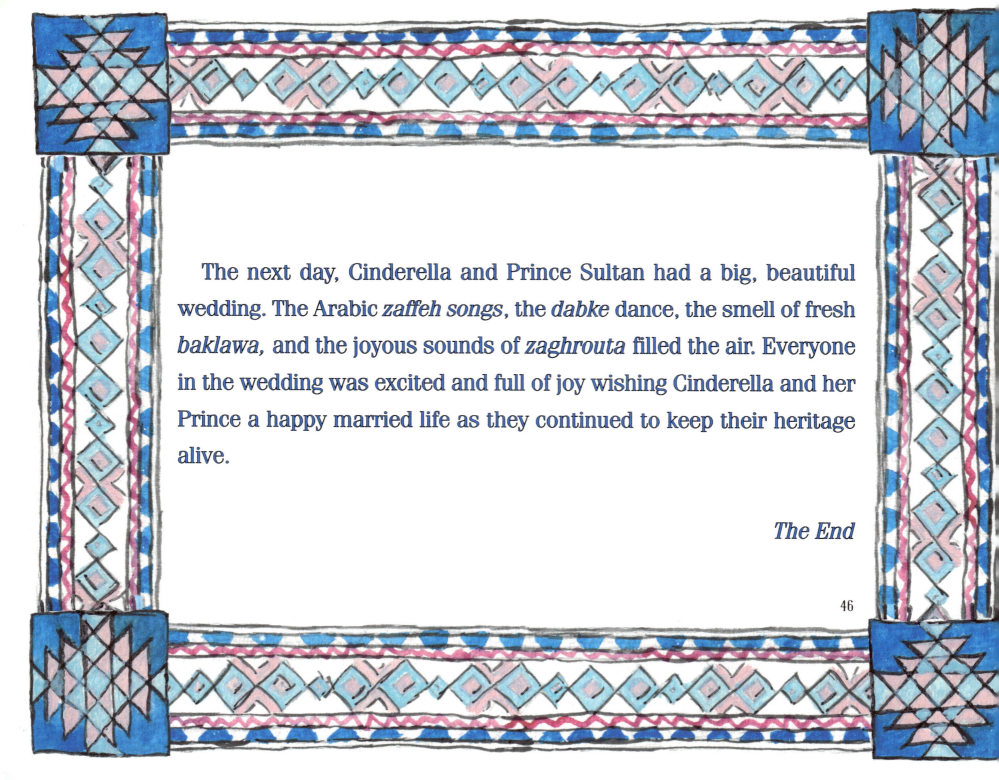

The next day, Cinderella and Prince Sultan had a big, beautiful wedding. The Arabic *zaffeh songs*, the *dabke* dance, the smell of fresh *baklawa,* and the joyous sounds of *zaghrouta* filled the air. Everyone in the wedding was excited and full of joy wishing Cinderella and her Prince a happy married life as they continued to keep their heritage alive.

The End

GLOSSARY

Check out the meanings of the Arabic words found in the story:

- Asal (عسل): An Arabic word that means "honey."
- Al-sadu (السدو): A type of embroidery hand-woven by Bedouin people. It is typically made from wool with a pattern of geometric shapes. It has recently been inscribed on the UNESCO list of Intangible Heritage.
- Dabke (دبكة): A native Levantine folk dance; it combines both circle and line dancing and is widely performed at weddings and joyous gatherings.
- Baklawa (بقلاوة): A Middle Eastern dessert made of paper-thin layers of pastry and chopped nuts.
- Eid (عيد): An Arabic term meaning "celebration." It is a religious holiday celebrated by Muslims worldwide.
- Eid Mubarak (عيد مبارك): An Eid greeting that means "blessed feast/festival."
- Henna (حناء): Powdered leaves used as a dye to color the hair and decorate hands for special occasions.
- Hijab (حجاب): A head covering/veil worn by Muslim women. It usually covers the head and chest.
- Jerash (جرش): An ancient city in northern Jordan.
- Petra (البتراء): An ancient city in Jordan, also called the "Rose City." It has been a UNESCO World Heritage Site since 1985.
- Ma'amoul (معمول): A cookie filled with fruits and nuts such as dates, walnuts, and pistachios. It is traditionally prepared for festivals and celebrations, such as Eids.
- Salam (سلام): A greeting in Arabic; it literally means "peace."
- Tabla (طبلة): A small hand-drum and beautifully decorated with wood.
- Zaffeh (زفة): Traditional wedding march that involves musical procession and folkloric dancing.
- Zaghrouta (زغروتة): A way to express happy emotions — A wavering and high-pitched sound representing trills of joy.

CPSIA information can be obtained
at www.ICGtesting.com
Printed in the USA
LVHW011224020723
750312LV00008B/46